This edition published by Parragon Books Ltd in 2017

Parragon Books Ltd
Chartist House
15–17 Trim Street
Bath BA1 1HA, UK
www.parragon.com

All stories based on the Marvel comic book series *The Avengers*.

Black Widow Bites Back! adapted by Elizabeth Schaefer. Illustrated by Neil Edwards and Rachelle Rosenberg.
Falcon Earns His Wings written by Scott Peterson. Illustrated by Andrea Di Vito and Rachelle Rosenberg.
Battle for Earth! written by Patrick Olliffe. Illustrated by Khoi Pham and Paul Mounts.
Arctic Attack! written by Frank Bumbalo. Illustrated by Khoi Pham and Paul Mounts.
Call for Backup written by Chris "Doc" Wyatt. Illustrated by Khoi Pham and Paul Mounts.
Thor Versus the Avengers written by Rebecca Schmidt. Illustrated by Wellinton Alvez and Rachelle Rosenberg.
Jurassic Central Park written by Tomas Palacios. Illustrated Agustin Padilla and Rachelle Rosenberg.
An Unexpected Hero written by Chris "Doc" Wyatt. Illustrated by Neil Edwards and Rachelle Rosenberg.

ISBN 978-1-4748-7342-0

Printed in China

Storybook
Collection

PaRragon

Bath • New York • Cologne • Melbourne • Delhi
Hong Kong • Shenzhen • Singapore

Contents

Black Widow Bites Back!

Natasha Romanoff and her brother, Alexi, were orphans. The two had been raised at the Red Room, an orphanage. Or was it?

Behind the scenes, the Red Room was home to a secret Russian spy programme. Which meant only one thing ... Natasha and Alexi became spies!

Together, they went on missions to gather information about S.H.I.E.L.D. But the two of them had just failed a recent assignment - again. Now they were waiting outside the office of the Red Room's leader, Ivan Bezukhov.

"This is all my fault," Alexi said. "Every time we've failed, it's because I messed up."

"Don't worry," Natasha reassured him. "I'll take care of you."

But Natasha was worried. They had made too many mistakes lately, and Ivan was not a patient man.

"You're so good at this spy stuff, Natasha," Alexi told his sister. "You're like a black widow. I'm like a clumsy hippo, ruining everything."

"Natasha." A cold voice came from behind them. It was Ivan. "I'll see you in my office now. Alone."

Natasha gave Alexi a smile, then stepped into Ivan's office.

"Today wasn't a good day for you, the Red Room, or – most importantly – me," Ivan said. "Alexi has been the cause of too many failed missions. He must be disposed of."

"No!" Natasha cried.

Natasha knew that the
Red Room disposed of failed
spies by wiping their memories.

"If you erase his memory,
he won't remember who *I* am,"
Natasha said. She couldn't
allow that to happen.

*I have to get Alexi out
of here!* She ran from Ivan's
office, but Red Room agents
were already dragging her
brother away.

Natasha fought her way
to freedom. She would find
a way to rescue Alexi.

She had to....

Natasha decided to go to the only people who could help – her old enemy, S.H.I.E.L.D. *I don't like this, but what choice do I have?*

Using her spy gear from the Red Room, Natasha reprogrammed an old S.H.I.E.L.D. identification badge to fool the security guards. Disguised as a cleaner, she sneaked into S.H.I.E.L.D. headquarters.

Natasha pushed her mop and bucket past a guard. Nothing – he didn't even glance at her. Once he was out of sight, she slipped into an air vent.

The vents were hot and airless, but a few twists and turns later, Natasha found herself directly above Director Nick Fury's office. Quietly, she slid open a vent door and – *whoosh!* – flipped her body down on to Fury's desk.

"What the...?" Before Fury could call security, Natasha begged him for his help – and his forgiveness.

"I know I've caused trouble for your team," Natasha quickly told Fury. "But I'll do anything S.H.I.E.L.D. asks. Just help me rescue my brother."

Fury reluctantly agreed. Natasha and Alexi *had* caused a lot of trouble, but....

"I can't leave you to the mercy of the Red Room," he muttered.

Fury set up a meeting with the Avengers. Natasha was surprised – they really wanted to help, even though none of them knew her.

"We'll rescue your brother," Captain America promised.

"Taking on the Red Room will be tricky, even for a super-spy like you, Natasha," Tony Stark added. "You'll need upgraded tech!"

That evening, Natasha led the Avengers to the Red Room's secret base.
The Avengers freed Ivan's prisoners as they searched the building for Alexi.

Suddenly, Natasha heard a familiar voice. "I see you've come home."
It was Ivan! The leader of the Red Room threw a vicious punch her way.

"Where is my brother?" Natasha asked, darting to block Ivan's fist.

Ivan gave a deep laugh. She tried to attack him, but he easily tackled
her every move. This was impossible!

"You can't hurt me," Ivan said.

Natasha thought quickly. "*I* can't, but I bet *this* will." She fired a powerful electric blast from her gauntlet. Instantly, Ivan collapsed to the ground.

"What was that?" Ivan cried, rolling over.

"An upgrade from Tony Stark. Now, where is my brother?"

There was no way Ivan could fight against the Avengers' technology. Climbing stiffly to his feet, he told Natasha where to find her brother.

Natasha rushed to Alexi's cell, but would she be too late?

The scene looked grim. Her brother was sprawled on the cell floor, his face like a death mask.

"Alexi!" she called.

His eyelids fluttered open. "What – what are you doing here? I thought Ivan had got rid of you...." he said.

"You're okay!" Natasha cried, rushing to hug her brother as the Avengers gathered around. She couldn't have saved Alexi without them.

Later, back at S.H.I.E.L.D. headquarters, Nick Fury took Natasha aside. "I don't know many spies who would have been able to break into my office. Or who would risk their lives for someone else," he said. "I would like you to join Earth's mightiest team of Super Heroes, the Avengers. What do you say, Natasha?"

"Count me in!" she said with a smile. "You can call me Black Widow."

Falcon Earns His Wings

F
alcon.

An invaluable member of the Avengers.

One of Captain America's best friends.

A brave hero who has saved the lives of Iron Man, Thor and Hulk.

But he hasn't always been this way.

Once upon a time, Falcon was just a boy named Sam Wilson.

Young Sam grew up in a tough neighbourhood of New York City.

His parents did their best to love him, protect him and teach him right from wrong.

Growing up, Sam felt a strong connection with birds. When his mum and dad saw this, they encouraged his love of animals and let him keep a pigeon coop on the roof of their flat.

But Sam lost his parents at an early age. Feeling hurt, scared and helpless, he decided the only way to survive was to become tougher and harder than anyone else.

Soon that was exactly what Sam was – tough! He did what it took to get ahead. But he always made sure to do what was right and stand up for others who felt as helpless as he once had.

To get a break from the city, Sam took a job on a strange island called the Isle of Exiles. But when he arrived, Sam discovered the island had been taken over by the evil Red Skull and his Hydra army!

Red Skull imprisoned Sam, wanting him to work for Hydra. Sam didn't take orders from anyone. He managed to escape, but not before Red Skull gave him the ability to communicate ... with birds!

Sam didn't run far.

He realized that there might be other people on the island who were being forced to work for Hydra. Sam decided to go back and free them!

But he couldn't do it alone. He needed a plan. Before he could think, there was a sudden noise coming from the jungle.

He followed the sounds and found a falcon trapped in a net. The bird wasn't hurt, but it was unable to free itself. Sam instantly felt a bond with the falcon and released it.

Sam named the falcon Redwing. He told the bird to take a message – quickly! – to anyone it could find.

Redwing returned with Captain America. Sam told Cap about Red Skull's evil plans.

There was no way they would let their enemy succeed! The two formed a plan to team up against the villainous Hydra.

But this was a dangerous mission. Sam needed to gear up. Captain America called S.H.I.E.L.D. agent Phil Coulson, and a special suit was delivered for Sam.

Falcon was born!

Along with Captain America and Redwing, he sneaked deep into the Isle of Exiles and freed the other prisoners.

Hydra was strong and powerful, but no match for such a mighty team. Even Red Skull's Cosmic Cube, which allowed him to bend the fabric of reality, could not save the Super Villain.

Working together, the heroes defeated Cap's most dangerous enemy.

Sam knew it was time to return to New York. He could not run from his pain. He had to face it.

But Sam was not the scared boy he had once been. As Falcon, he could help make New York a safer place.

Falcon often partnered with Captain America, and S.H.I.E.L.D. even made him a set of artificial wings that enabled him to fly.

Now Sam really was like a falcon!

Falcon proved himself time and again. Eventually, he was invited to join the Avengers.

Earth's Mightiest Heroes gained a strong and loyal new member. And Falcon found a family at last.

Battle for Earth!

It was a quiet night. The Avengers were enjoying a well-deserved rest when – *BOOM!* – an explosion rocked the Natural History Museum.

The Avengers rushed to the scene. There they were met with the sight of Thanos – one of the most dangerous villains in the universe.

Thanos was searching for an ancient artefact – the magical Sword of Histria. No one was going to stop him!

The Super Villain fired a blast at Captain America using his Infinity Gauntlet, a magic glove that drew its energy from six powerful gems.

Captain America quickly raised his indestructible shield. But Thanos was powerful. The force of his blast threw Captain America backwards into his fellow Avenger, Falcon.

"You humans are no match for me," the villain bellowed as he moved deeper into the museum. "Once I have the Sword of Histria, I will slice your beloved planet Earth in two!"

Hawkeye moved into position to stop the Super Villain, but Thanos was faster than the hero had imagined. Before Hawkeye could even lift his bow, Thanos spun round and blasted the archer off his feet!

Swivelling back round, Thanos smashed the glass case that protected the Sword of Histria.

He laughed as he grasped the magical artefact.

"The Sword is mine!" he roared. "My plan is almost complete. No one will be able to get in my way now."

Captain America and Black Widow charged towards Thanos, determined that he wouldn't escape with the Sword, but they were too late. Light glowed around him and they were thrown back.

Raising the glowing Sword above his head, the Super Villain teleported away, leaving Cap and Black Widow gazing at an empty space. They'd failed.

All that was left to do was tend to an injured Hawkeye and Falcon.

High above the ground, hidden among the clouds, hovered the massive S.H.I.E.L.D. helicarrier, headquarters of the world's best super-spies.

On board, the Avengers held an emergency meeting with Nick Fury, the director of S.H.I.E.L.D.

"We know why Thanos stole the Sword of Histria and what his ultimate plan is," Captain America told the group. "But we don't know where he's going."

"According to intel on the Sword, it's powerless unless it's returned to the place it was created," Iron Man said.

Nick Fury shook his head. "That could be anywhere."

Just as they were feeling beyond hope, Special Agent Ruby, who specialized in ancient artefacts, joined the group.

"I can help," Agent Ruby said. "The Sword was being held for safekeeping at the Natural History Museum, but my sources say it was created at Castle Aarole in the Carpathian Mountains."

On a tablet, Agent Ruby pulled up an image of the castle.

Nick Fury glanced at the screen, then turned to the group. He gave them a grim smile. "Looks like you're going to Romania."

The Avengers didn't waste a moment. They boarded the Quinjet and raced to Romania.

The heroes soon arrived at Castle Aarole. But Thanos had beaten them there. As the Avengers rushed towards him, the Sword of Histria began to glow with ancient energy. It was very close to the place it had been forged.

The Avengers had to stop Thanos fast. They were the planet's last hope! The team sprang into action, but it was clear Thanos wasn't going down without a fight.

Thor and Hulk kept attacking. Thor threw his enchanted hammer, Mjolnir, at Thanos – *SMACK!* Hulk smashed his fists into the ground – *CRASH!* Shock waves radiated out, shaking the earth beneath their feet.

But Thanos had drawn extra energy from the Sword of Histria. He was more powerful than ever and easily deflected Thor's hammer. Even the tremors Hulk's giant fists had created couldn't make him lose his footing.

As the Sword pulsed with magical energy, Thanos easily stepped over the crumbled outer wall of the castle. Just a few more feet and the Sword would be back near the forge where it was created, and back at full power.

Iron Man raced in to stop Thanos, but the Super Villain used the power of the Sword to short-circuit Iron Man's armour. As Thanos strode forwards, he fired an energy blast at Hulk. The blast would only temporarily blind Hulk, but Thanos knew it would give him the time he needed.

With Hulk out of the way, Thanos swept past the rest of the Avengers and into the ancient castle.

Behind him, Black Widow fired electrostatic bolts from her bracelets. But she was too late! The energy had no effect on the Super Villain. Thanos had reached his ultimate destination – the spot where the Sword of Histria had been created so many centuries earlier.

As Thanos raised the Sword triumphantly in the air, a swirl of bright light filled the sky above him. The Avengers threw their hands up to protect their eyes. The colours were blinding! The blaze of energy engulfed Thanos and the mystical Sword.

The ground shook beneath the Avengers' feet. The air, charged with magical power, crackled around them. Had Thanos won?

The Avengers needed another plan....

Iron Man's armour was useless, but Tony Stark's genius-level mind was not. He had a plan. They couldn't defeat Thanos as long as he had the Sword. But they *could* destroy the Sword itself.

Thor used Mjolnir to summon lightning and charge Cap's shield with Asgardian energy.

Iron Man turned to Hulk. "We need your strength," he said.

Without hesitation, Hulk hurled the energized shield at the Sword of Histria.

Thanos gazed in awe at the Sword. Any moment now, he'd be empowered to slice the Earth in two. But suddenly a red, white and blue blur zoomed towards him. An attack! It was too late to deflect.

Captain America's shield, powered by Thor's Asgardian energy and Hulk's superhuman strength, struck the Sword of Histria. Thanos leaped back, but he could not keep his grasp on the weapon. The magical artefact shattered into a thousand pieces.

The Sword's ancient energies flew out in an explosion that knocked Thanos to the ground. Pieces of the precious Sword fell around him.

Thanos knew he was defeated. His stolen Sword was shattered and so were his plans for the destruction of Earth.

The triumphant Avengers surrounded Thanos, but the Super Villain quickly teleported away in a flash of energized mist. They should have known he wouldn't allow himself to be captured.

What the Avengers did know was that Thanos would return one day. He'd try to finish what he'd started. When he did, Earth's Mightiest Heroes would be there to stop him!

Arctic Attack!

The Avengers were safely back at base after a dangerous mission. But there would be no rest for this weary team of Super Heroes. Captain America had called a meeting to go over recent world events – much to the dismay of his exhausted allies.

"Cap, can we speed this along?" Hawkeye yawned. The warm meeting room made it difficult to keep his eyes open. "If we're not going to be out there fighting bad guys, I'd like to get some rest."

"Have patience, Hawkeye," Captain America said. "You never know when we'll be needed – or where."

As if on cue, the Avengers' emergency alarm began to ring!

"Come in, Avengers. This is Matthew Woods from NORAD. I'm calling from the Arctic Ocean. We have an emergency! Can you hear me?"

"We can hear you loud and clear, Matthew," Iron Man responded. "What's wrong?"

"It's the polar ice caps, Avengers," Matthew said. "There's something strange going on."

"Are they melting quicker than usual?" Falcon asked.

"No, just the opposite," Matthew said. "The ice is spreading at an extreme rate. If we don't stop it soon, it will engulf the whole northern hemisphere. The world is in grave danger."

The Avengers knew there wasn't a moment to lose. They rushed
to the Quinjet and launched themselves towards the Arctic Ocean.
When they arrived at the top of the world, the Avengers were shocked
by what they saw. Mountains of ice were erupting from the Arctic!

"Get us on the ground – fast," Cap told Black Widow. But before she
could react, the temperature outside the Quinjet suddenly dropped –
and so did the Quinjet!

"Brace yourselves, Avengers!" Black Widow screamed as the Quinjet spun out of control. "We are coming in hot!"

Iron Man, Falcon and Thor tried their best to steady the Quinjet, but their powers were no match for the frigid ice storm. With a thuddering jolt, the Quinjet crashed into a massive snowbank.

"What caused the temperature to drop so fast?" Falcon asked as the escape hatch opened. The heroes scrambled out.

"Not what, friend Falcon – who. Look to the tallest iceberg to find your answer," Thor replied.

Falcon and the rest of the Avengers looked up the wall of ice to see the Frost Giants of Jotunheim.

"The Jotuns are the villains behind this deadly ice," Thor continued as lightning began to crackle all around him. "Steadfast, Avengers, they are vile creatures."

"Ah, the son of Odin. We have been waiting for you," called Laufey, king of the Jotuns.

Laufey's eyes were as cold and blue as the frozen sky above, and his voice shook the snow-packed ground. "How do you like the work we are doing to this human world, your precious Midgard?" he continued.

Thor tightened his grip on his hammer, Mjolnir. "Laufey, cease your actions at once and return to your rightful realm in Jotunheim," he said through gritted teeth. "I shall not warn you again."

"We shall not return, Odinson. Earth will be our home now," Laufey said as the ice and snow swirled around him. "The Asgardians destroyed our world. Your father himself led the attack, and what Odin took from the Jotuns, we shall take from his son!"

The snow storm suddenly intensified, making it hard for the Avengers to see or breathe. The Jotun twins, Lok and Hagen, brandished their massive clubs and, as one, charged towards Thor.

"Avengers, assemble!" Captain America shouted.

The Avengers fought with all their might, but their frozen bodies were no match for the combined threat of the Frost Giants and the swirling storm that surrounded them.

"Cap!" Iron Man yelled into his comlink. "I have a plan, but I have to get back to the Quinjet. Can you keep them distracted, then round them up when I give the signal?"

"Will do, but make it quick," Captain America gasped. "I don't know how much longer we can hold them off – or survive in this ice storm!"

Iron Man didn't waste a moment. He flew into the Quinjet, signalling for Hulk to go with him. Hulk retreated to the jet while the Jotuns called down yet more snow and ice around them.

"Hulk," Iron Man began. "I need you to rip out the cargo bay doors. They are made of aluminium." He smiled. "It's a great conductor of electricity."

As Hulk tugged the metal doors, Iron Man spoke into his comlink again.

"Avengers, listen up. We have to round up the Jotuns. Get them close together so that Hulk and I can wrap them in aluminium. Then it's Thor's turn to bring the thunder – and the lightning!"

As the rest of the Avengers put Iron Man's plan into action,
Thor stamped Mjolnir on the ground and called down the lightning.
Together, the Avengers directed the lightning to electrify the Jotuns.
At last! The deadly storm faded away to mere snowflakes.

Defeated, the Frost Giants fell to the ground. "Thank you, friends," Thor said to his teammates. "I will take the Jotuns to the dungeon of Asgard." He called to Heimdall to open the Rainbow Bridge.

As the Rainbow Bridge opened, Cap turned to a shivering Hawkeye. "Bet you wish you were in a warm meeting room now," he said.

"I sure do!" Hawkeye replied. "I've had enough of the Jotuns, and enough snow, to last me a lifetime!"

Call for Backup

Billionaire inventor Tony Stark loved new technology. His company, Stark Industries, had been hard at work on a new spaceship that could safely take groups of tourists to the moon. Finally, it was ready for its maiden flight.

In his Iron Man armour, Tony proudly flew alongside the ship as it blasted off.

Only a short time later, Iron Man greeted the ship's passengers at the new Stark Industries Moon Base. Iron Man had invited influential people, including international leaders in government and business, to be part of the first privileged group to visit the base.

As introductions were still going on, the tourists' fun was interrupted by a huge flash of light and a crash.

"Don't worry," Iron Man assured the group. "It's probably nothing dangerous. I'll go and check it out."

But secretly, Iron Man was worried. *What could have caused that crash?* he wondered as he rocketed towards the site.

Iron Man called his teammates, the Avengers, to help.

"We're in the middle of a battle with Hydra," said Captain America over the communicator. "We'll get there as soon as we can, but it could take a while."

For now, Iron Man was on his own!

Iron Man was right to be worried. A familiar figure emerged from the crash site. Thanos! He was an evil ruler from deep space who wanted nothing more than to take over Earth.

Thanos wasn't alone. He had brought along his army of Outriders – a race of alien warriors, each with four strong arms, long claws and razor-sharp teeth.

Iron Man was in serious trouble. With the Avengers occupied, he called the only other group that might be able to help.

Deep in space, on the bridge of their mighty starship, the Guardians of the Galaxy received Iron Man's distress call.

"Tony Stark's in big trouble," reported Star-Lord, the brave leader of the Guardians.

"Let's go," said the alien soldier, Drax.

"How can we get there in time?" asked green-skinned Gamora. "We're halfway across the galaxy!"

"I am Groot," remarked the plant creature, Groot.

"Good point, Groot," said Rocket Raccoon, a small but skilled mercenary. Groot only ever said "I am Groot", but Rocket always knew what he meant. "Groot thinks we should ask the Nova Corps for a boost."

Star-Lord radioed the Nova Corps, a group of interstellar peacekeepers. "We need an emergency teleport to Earth's moon," he said.

Happy to help, the Novas quickly initiated a teleportation beam that flew the Guardians through space.

As soon as the Guardians arrived, they leaped into the fight.

"What took you so long?" asked Iron Man, pinned to the ground by the Outriders.

"We come all the way from the other side of the galaxy, and this is the thanks we get?" asked Rocket.

"I am Groot," added Groot.

"Time for battle!" yelled Gamora, smashing the Outriders.

"Guardians, don't hold back on these guys," ordered Star-Lord.

Forced to fight the Guardians, the Outriders backed off from Iron Man.

The armoured Avenger leaped up to help defend against further attacks.

"You sure know how to get into trouble, Stark," joked Rocket.

While the Guardians and Iron Man were fighting the Outriders, Thanos strode towards the moon base.

Iron Man suddenly understood Thanos's plan.

"He must be trying to capture everyone at the base," Iron Man said. "So many of Earth's important leaders are gathered there. Thanos could grab them all at once."

Robbed of its greatest leaders, the planet would be vulnerable. Thanos could easily invade and proclaim himself the new ruler.

But Thanos didn't get far, because … the Avengers had arrived, and
not a moment too soon! They leaped out of their Quinjet.

"Avengers, assemble!" ordered Captain America, directing the team
in combat.

"That's right. If you want a shot at Earth, you'll have to go through
us first," Hawkeye called to Thanos.

"Hulk smash!" yelled battle-ready Hulk, racing towards their enemy.

The Avengers brought together their combined powers and abilities to stop Thanos.

"Have at thee, villain!" Thor shouted, hurling his mighty hammer.

"That goes for all of us," Falcon agreed as he swooped in.

"We will stop you, Thanos," promised Black Widow.

But despite all their combined might, Thanos was still gaining ground.

Iron Man scanned Thanos and discovered something new.

"That device at his belt – he's never had that before," he said.

"Could that machine be what helped Thanos travel here?"

Thanos had arrived on the moon in a huge crash. But Iron Man didn't see a ship anywhere and Thanos was unharmed. He must have used some new technology.

Quickly, Iron Man formed a plan. He needed Groot. The little plant creature held some big secrets.

"I'm going to need your special talents here, buddy," Iron Man said to Groot.

"I am Groot," replied Groot.

"You bet you are!" agreed Iron Man.

Iron Man flew Groot over
Thanos and dropped him
right into the middle of
the fight.

"Bombs away!" the
armoured Avenger shouted.

As he fell, Groot
transformed from a little
plant into a giant plant.

"What is this?"
demanded Thanos, as Groot
appeared out of nowhere.

"I am Groot!" Groot
yelled, delivering blow after
crushing blow to Thanos.

Thanos was so distracted by Groot's sudden attack that he didn't notice Iron Man swoop in and steal the device from his belt.

Quickly studying the device, Iron Man worked out how to reverse its effects. He pressed a button and a glowing orb of energy formed around Thanos and the Outriders.

With another push of a button, Iron Man sent the villains shooting away from the surface of the moon.

"Nooooo!" Thanos cried as he catapulted away.

"Where are you sending them, Tony?" asked Captain America.

"Back to where they came from," responded Iron Man. "And robbed of this device, we won't see them back here anytime soon."

Back on the moon base, Earth's leaders and their families were happy to be safe from Thanos and excited to meet their heroes. Thanks to the Avengers and their friends, the Guardians of the Galaxy, the trip to the moon would go down as a great success, and Earth was safe once again!

Thor Versus the Avengers

It was a bright, sunny day in New York City. Captain America and Black Widow were patrolling when they received an urgent call from S.H.I.E.L.D. about a disturbance downtown.

Cap and Black Widow raced to the scene. They arrived to find an entire army of charging Asgardians. Leading them was Thor!

"There must be a big problem for Thor to think we need all these Asgardians," Captain America said to Black Widow.

Black Widow looked around. "I don't know. This feels strange, Captain," she said.

Suddenly, they heard a man cry out. "Help! Captain America! The aliens are going to attack us!"

Cap realized that Thor and the Asgardians were the disturbance S.H.I.E.L.D. had called him about. "Thor!" Captain America yelled. "What's going on?"

Thor didn't answer. Instead, he signalled the Asgardians to intensify their attack!

Captain America and Black Widow had no choice. They would have to defend Earth's people against the Asgardian army. Captain America sliced his shield through the air to knock a sword out of an enemy warrior's hand. Before it hit the ground, Black Widow caught the sword and smashed the hilt into another Asgardian.

"We need help!" Black Widow yelled as she signalled to Hawkeye, who had just arrived with Hulk.

But Hawkeye wasn't paying attention to her. He and the Incredible Hulk had followed a separate army of Asgardians into an abandoned warehouse.

"Smash!" Hulk yelled.

"Shhh, Hulk. We're trying to sneak up on them!" said Hawkeye. "What's wrong with them? I wish Thor was here."

Suddenly, Hawkeye heard a noise behind him and spun round, drawing an arrow out of his quiver. It was Thor!

"Thor? I almost shot you!" Hawkeye said.

"Smash!" Hulk shouted, running towards Thor.

"Hulk, what are you doing? That's our friend!" Hawkeye said. But Thor still wasn't saying anything. "Thor...?"

Hulk charged at Thor, but his body tore through thin air. The Asgardian was an illusion! The green Goliath smashed into a support beam. Walls shook and the ceiling cracked. The building was falling down around them!

Meanwhile, high in the air, Iron Man and Falcon saw the building begin to crumble. They flew over as fast as they could. "Quick, we have to get in there and help them!" Falcon said.

"Already on it," Iron Man said, zooming past Falcon. The pair reached the warehouse just in time to pull Hawkeye out of the wreckage. Luckily, Hulk had managed to hold up enough of the building to keep his teammate safe.

"It was … it was Thor!"

But it wasn't Thor. At least, not the real Thor. The Asgardian had heard the sirens, too, and flew downtown to see what was happening.

When Thor arrived, he was shocked to see an entire troop of Asgardians attacking a bridge of trapped civilians.

"Brothers, what are you doing here?" Thor asked, landing on the bridge. Their only answer was a flash of their swords.

"Run!" Thor told the civilians, but they seemed just as afraid of him as their attackers. What was going on? Why were the Asgardians attacking, and why were the civilians so frightened of Thor? He had to help the civilians get away, but Thor didn't want to hurt his own people.

Before the Asgardians could reach Thor, he slammed Mjolnir against the bridge. The shock wave knocked out the warriors.

Thor knew something was wrong. He needed the Avengers.

Suddenly, Thor heard more shouts coming from beneath the bridge. A group of civilians were pointing at the sky.

Thor raised Mjolnir and turned to see … himself?

Now Thor *really* knew something strange was happening. How could there be two of him?

"What is this trickery?" Thor asked.

His double gave a thin smile.

Thor realized it was time he got to the bottom of this mystery. With a roar, he called down a huge lightning bolt. The sky grew dark and crackled with energy. Thor pointed his hammer at his foe.

The bolt of lightning hit the other Thor, who disappeared!

Thor heard a slow clap and a low laugh behind him. He turned round to find a villain grinning at him. It was his mischievous brother, Loki.

"Brother, it has been a long time," Thor said.

"Not long enough," Loki replied.

"What are you doing?" Thor asked.

"I'm robbing Earth of one of its so-called heroes!" Loki answered. "When this world sees you and your Asgardian army attacking innocent civilians, they will never trust you again. You'll be an exile, just as you have forced me to be."

Thor realized that his double must have been one of Loki's mirages. He couldn't believe his brother would go to such lengths to hurt him. Thor needed to turn the Asgardian army to his side.

"I have all the Asgardians under my control," Loki said, as if reading Thor's mind. "They won't help you!"

"The Avengers...." Thor began.

"They won't help you, either. With my Thor mirages, I've made sure they'll never trust you again!" Loki said, sneering.

"You underestimate us, Brother. The Avengers trust each other. We will not be broken up by one of your tricks!" Thor said.

"What a fool you are," Loki laughed. "Where are your friends now?"

"Right here," said a voice. It was Iron Man!

Loki turned round, shocked! Iron Man, Captain America, Hulk, Black Widow, Hawkeye and Falcon were all right behind him.

"But ... but," Loki stammered, for once at a loss for words.

"You will not win this day, Loki. Surrender, and let us end this," Thor said.

"How is this possible?" Loki asked the Avengers.

"I trust my friends," Thor said.

"And we trust you, buddy," Captain America said. "We knew as soon as Fake Thor began attacking us that there had to be some sort of explanation!"

But Loki was not going to give up. He raised his staff and gave the signal to – attack! The army of Asgardians lunged towards them.

While the rest of the Avengers fought to knock out the Asgardians, Thor ran towards Loki. He knew that his brother's staff must be the source of this evil, keeping his people under Loki's command. If he could break it, the Asgardians would be set free.

Thor summoned a bolt of lightning, but Loki easily deflected it back on his brother. Its force hurled Thor back against a nearby building.

The mighty Mjolnir flew out of Thor's hands and he slumped to the ground.

"I've defeated you again, Brother," Loki said. "The Asgardians will continue to attack, and there is no way to stop them." He turned to walk away.

"Never," Thor said, raising his hand to summon Mjolnir. As the mighty hammer flew towards Thor, it smashed into Loki's staff, breaking it in two!

Suddenly, the Asgardians stopped fighting. With Loki's staff broken, they were now free of his control. The warriors surrounded Loki. He could not escape!

"I'll return, Thor," Loki said as the Asgardians dragged him away.

The Avengers assembled around Thor. As people cheered, Thor smiled. Thor was a hero again and the Avengers were a team once more.

Together, they would continue to fight to protect the world!

Jurassic Central Park

It had been a long week for the mighty Avengers. First they had taken on the Jotuns. Then they had battled Thanos and the Outriders. Now it was time to rest!

Dr Bruce Banner and billionaire inventor Tony Stark were enjoying a lazy day in Tony's lab, where Tony kept all of his cool gadgets and inventions.

"So ... wanna build something?" Tony asked Bruce.

Bruce shrugged. "Sure. But something small."

Three hours later, Nick Fury burst into Tony's lab. "Stark!" he yelled. "What did you do?"

Fury pointed at a massive portal that was opening in Central Park.

Tony cringed. "We may have built a teeny, tiny ... time machine."

"You built a time machine?" Fury yelled. "To what period?"

Before Tony could answer,
a huge silhouette emerged
from the portal. Several figures
followed. *Lots* of figures, in fact!

Terrifying tyrannosaurs,
velociraptors with razor-sharp
teeth and pterodactyls with
winged claws all rushed through.
With slathering jaws, they roared
at everything in their way.
The time machine had opened
a portal to ... the Jurassic period!

"I'm not one to tattle," Tony
said, "but Bruce helped."

Fury leaned in. "Then I would
get him mad ... and quick!"

Tony pulled on his Iron Man armour and rocketed towards the menacing carnivores. But he wasn't alone. The Incredible Hulk was right behind him!

"I wish Falcon was here," said Iron Man, firing a repulsor beam at an incoming pterodactyl. "Maybe he can speak their language."

"Hulk speak language!" the green Goliath said as he rammed into a T. Rex. "Hulk *ROAR!*"

As more and more dinosaurs came through the portal, the battle quickly turned disastrous.

Hulk tried to stay on top, but he was overpowered when a group of dinosaurs attacked him from all sides.

Iron Man struggled with a raptor that was crushing his armour in its mighty jaw!

"You know," Iron Man cried as he ducked to avoid the raptor's razor-sharp claws, "this ... isn't ... going as planned!"

"Remind me to never, ever play with Pym's particle beam again!"
Iron Man said. "I knew crossing those wires would create a portal
to another time ... but I was hoping for the seventies!"

Just as it looked like the T. rex would finally take down Hulk,
a powerful force whizzed by and sent them both flying across
the park.

"What was —" Iron Man began, but before he could finish, something flew past him, too. A loud explosion knocked a pterodactyl out of the sky and a blast sent the raptors tumbling to the ground.

"'Bout time you showed up!" Iron Man said with a smile.

It was the other mighty Avengers!

Iron Man shook Captain America's hand. "Hey, Cap," he said. "Let me guess, Fury told you about our tiny issue with a couple of lizards?"

"Tiny?" Cap repeated, looking up at a roaring T. rex.

Thor stepped forward. "Let's even the score. What say you?"

Hulk grinned. "I SAY YOU!"

The Avengers launched themselves into the fray. With a few repulsor blasts from Iron Man, some trick shots from Hawkeye and a couple of Black Widow's bites, the Avengers backed the monsters into the portal. Thor hurled his mighty hammer, Mjolnir, at a T. rex, sending it stumbling back to its prehistoric world.

"Hulk has idea!" the green Avenger said as he tore a metal fence that surrounded a nearby park out of the ground.

"As long as the idea isn't eating or keeping them!" Iron Man joked.

Hulk wrapped the metal fencing around a bunch of raptors and sealed them in tight. He spun them around and around, then hurled them back into the portal, which snapped closed behind them. With a loud sucking noise, the portal disappeared into the air.

The Avengers had saved Central Park – and Iron Man and Hulk, too!

The next day, after the Avengers cleaned up the city, Tony Stark and Bruce Banner tidied Tony's lab.

Tony looked at Bruce and grinned. "Hey ... wanna see who can pick up Thor's hammer or throw Cap's shield the farthest?"

Bruce shook his head. "You just don't learn your lesson, do you?" he said. Then he smiled. "Okay. Hit me!"

An Unexpected Hero

Agent Phil Coulson was in his office aboard S.H.I.E.L.D.'s top-secret plane when a call came in from his boss, Nick Fury.

"I'm sending you to Egypt, Coulson," Fury said. "There are strange signals coming from some long-abandoned ruins and I need you to check them out."

Coulson nodded. "Yes, sir. I'll have the plane change course at once," he replied.

Coulson arrived at the ruins and turned on the plane's scanners.

Something was very wrong. The energy readings were off the charts.

Agent Coulson left the plane and carefully approached the ruins.

Hidden behind a pile of ancient bricks was a strange door.

Coulson ducked through the door and looked around. He expected to see a dusty tomb or a library full of old scrolls. Instead, he found a high-tech lab.

Agent Coulson studied the unusual equipment. "These systems are so advanced," he whispered. "I've never seen anything like them."

"That's because I invented them," a voice said. It was Ultron.

"Welcome, Agent Coulson," Ultron said with a laugh. "I was hoping you would join me."

Agent Coulson backed away, trying to find an escape route, but he was trapped. The robotic Super Villain was blocking the only exit.

"I don't know what you're planning, Ultron," Coulson began, "but –"

Suddenly, Coulson found he couldn't talk. Ultron had hurled a disc at him that froze his body in place.

This was bad.

Meanwhile, in New York, the Avengers were finishing a battle against A.I.M., a group of evil scientists bent on ruling the world.

"Come on, guys. A doom ray?" taunted Iron Man. "How unimaginative. I thought you A.I.M. guys would do better than that!"

The words were barely out
of his mouth, when a large figure
appeared in the sky above
the Avengers.

"Isn't that your Hulkbuster
armour?" Falcon asked Iron Man.
Iron Man had designed a special
armoured suit that was as
tough as Hulk himself.

"Ha," sneered Hulk. "Puny
armour. Hulk is strongest one
there is."

"We know that, big guy,"
Iron Man assured Hulk.
"But that is one of my suits.
What's it doing here?"

Before anyone could answer, the Hulkbuster armour suddenly attacked them.

"Look out!" Captain America cried, raising his shield.

The Hulkbuster landed beside Thor, who reached up and ripped off its helmet. Inside was a gagged Agent Coulson.

Iron Man tore away the gag. "What are you doing in my suit?" he asked the agent.

"Ultron froze me with a strange disc and then shoved me inside," Coulson explained, panting. "I've been trapped in here for hours."

"Don't worry, Coulson, we'll get you out of there," Iron Man assured the agent. "I just need to get you back to my armoury. Hulk?"

Hulk grunted and picked up the suit. With Coulson over his shoulder, he followed the other Avengers to Iron Man's armoury. Inside were all the suits Iron Man had created over the years.

Iron Man plugged
Coulson and the Hulkbuster
armour into his computer.
Almost immediately, a loud
alarm started to sound.

"The armour has
uploaded some kind of
computer virus into the
armoury's systems,"
Iron Man cried.

"That's right, Stark,"
a voice announced. It was
Ultron! He had followed
Coulson back to New York
and tracked him all the way
to Iron Man's armoury.

"You fools are so predictable," Ultron said. "I knew you would bring your agent here to free him."

Iron Man strode across to a control panel and pushed a button. Nothing happened.

Ultron laughed. "My virus has hijacked your computer system," he said. "Your armoury belongs to me."

Ultron raised his hand in the direction of the suits. Iron Man's entire collection rose into the air.

"And now, Avengers, let's see how you do against not one, but an *army* of Iron Men," screamed Ultron.

The empty suits circled in the air to surround the heroes. Then, at Ultron's command, they launched an attack.

From inside the Hulkbuster, Agent Coulson watched the Avengers battle the empty suits.

I should be out there fighting with them! he thought.

"These mere empty shells cannot defeat us," cried Thor as he pounded one of the heavier suits with his hammer.

"Especially not when we work together," agreed Captain America. "Avengers, assemble!"

Working together, the Avengers broke apart one suit after another.

"You see, Ultron," said Iron Man, "even when we're outnumbered, the Avengers will always defeat evil."

Ultron laughed. "Once again, you did just as I had hoped. Thank you for saving me the trouble of breaking these suits apart myself."

Ultron raised his hand again, and the pieces of armour that were scattered throughout the room flew towards him. One by one, the pieces attached to his metal body – making him bigger, stronger and more powerful than ever!

"Behold *Mega-Ultron*," shouted Ultron, "the greatest robot of all time."

The Avengers battled bravely against the new, improved Ultron – but he was too strong.

"I can't believe it," cried Hawkeye. "Even with all of us fighting him, he's still winning."

Behind them, unnoticed, Iron Man's computer continued to work. Suddenly, there was a faint *click* and the Hulkbuster armour popped open.

Agent Coulson reached into the armour and picked up the disc that Ultron had used to freeze him. *Maybe I can use Ultron's own plan against him,* he thought.

With Ultron distracted, Coulson climbed the armour racks to a spot above the giant robot. It was a big risk, but ... taking a deep breath, he leaped towards Ultron.

Coulson reached out with the disc and – *BAM!* – it attached to Ultron, who instantly froze in place!

"Smart thinking, son of Coul," Thor said. "You tricked Ultron. Very Loki of you."

"I'm glad I was able to help," said Coulson, dusting down his suit.

"If you want to help, come up here and get all these pieces off Ultron," shouted Iron Man. "I hope you're good at jigsaw puzzles, because we need to fix *all* of my suits."

As he pieced together the Iron Man suits, Coulson smiled to himself. He was proud to fight beside the Avengers and call them friends.

The End